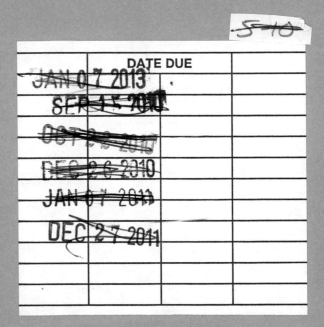

DATE DUE		
JAN 0 7 2013		
SEP 15 2010		
OCT 2010		
DEC 26 2010		
JAN 07 2011		
DEC 27 2011		

Corkscrew Counts

a story about multiplication

Donna Jo Napoli and Richard Tchen
pictures by Anna Currey

HENRY HOLT AND COMPANY • NEW YORK

Henry Holt and Company, LLC
Publishers since 1866
175 Fifth Avenue
New York, New York 10010
www.HenryHoltKids.com

Library of Congress Cataloging-in-Publication Data
Napoli, Donna Jo.
Corkscrew counts : a story about multiplication
Donna Jo Napoli and Richard Tchen ; illustrated by Anna Currey.—1st ed.
p.   cm.
Summary: Corkscrew the pig is celebrating his birthday, but as his owners and their
friends form various groups to play games, they leave out Corkscrew and his new friend,
Pirate the parrot, who make it clear they want to join in the fun.
ISBN-13: 978-0-8050-7664-6 / ISBN-10: 0-8050-7664-6
[1. Birthdays—Fiction. 2. Parties—Fiction. 3. Pigs—Fiction. 4. Parrots—Fiction.
5. Multiplication—Fiction.] I. Tchen, Richard. II. Currey, Anna, ill. III. Title.
PZ7.N15Cor 2008   [E]—dc22   2007040034

First Edition—2008
Printed in China on acid-free paper. ∞
1 3 5 7 9 10 8 6 4 2

For Boots and Panther and all those birds
Love, Donna Jo and Richard

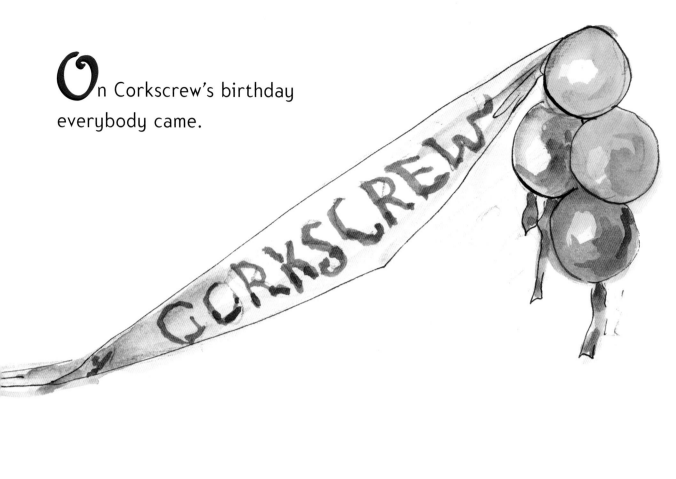

On Corkscrew's birthday
everybody came.

Two friends for little Joey.
Two friends for Petey.
And two friends each for the twins, Sally and
Samantha.

"Come get your presents, Corkscrew," called Sally.

Corkscrew eyed the four children in his family and the eight extra kids. All twelve grinned at him. It would be okay to go back inside, except for that scary parrot.

Still, presents were presents. A dozen of them! And this was his first party ever. He didn't want to disappoint his guests.

The kids helped Corkscrew open the presents. Booties? Booties were for sissies, every pig knew that. And who would he walk on that leash? This stuff looked like toys for cats and dogs. Didn't they know he was a pig?

But at least the paper was good. He nibbled
on the wrapping and ate a bow.

"Do you like bows, Corkscrew? Mine's pretty."
"Let's dress him up!"
The kids tied the rest of the bows on Corkscrew.
Then they looked around. "What now?"

Petey pulled on Sally's arm. "Yeah, this was your idea. What do we do at a pig's birthday party?"

"What you do at any party."

"Play dress-up?"

"No. Play games. Then eat."

One kid picked a deck of cards off the coffee table. He shuffled, then spread them out for solitaire.

The others gave him advice.

"Me, too," said Joey.

"We all want to play."

"We all need cards."

Everybody searched the living room.

"Wait a minute," said Samantha. "If each person plays alone, we need twelve decks. And I know we don't have that many."

1 x 12 = 12

They all went back to standing around the one kid who had the cards.

Corkscrew wiggled through the ring and snuffled up a card. It wasn't as tasty as the bow.

"Squawk!" The parrot flapped his wings. Cards flew.

Corkscrew shook the cards off his back. Hey, maybe that bird wasn't such a bore.

"Bad Corkscrew!"

"Bad Pirate!"

"Now we don't even have one full deck."

"Solitaire stinks anyway. How about games we can play with each other?"

"You mean, like in pairs?"

"Sure. There are twelve of us, so we have six pairs."

"How about badminton?"

2 x 6 = 12

"Let's go out to the garage."

Two kids grabbed badminton rackets and a birdie.

"Are there enough for all of us to play?"

"Yeah. We've got exactly six pairs of rackets and six birdies."

Corkscrew picked up a racket. Pirate caught a birdie. Pretty nice work, thought Corkscrew. That parrot might even be fun.

"Bad Corkscrew!"

"Bad Pirate!"

"Now one racket's slimy with pig slobber, and we're short a birdie."

"Going in pairs wasn't such a hot idea anyway because we're all different sizes. We've got three little kids, three medium kids, and six big kids. Let's play a game in four groups of three."

3 x 4 = 12

"Look in this basket. Jump ropes! And there are four of them. We can all take turns swinging and jumping."

Corkscrew got tangled in a rope. Pirate did loop-the-loops in another. Corkscrew watched with admiration.

"Bad Corkscrew!"

"Bad Pirate!"

"We can't keep jumping or Corkscrew and
Pirate will get hurt."

"Besides, the little kids can't swing or jump
good. What else can we play?"

"I want to play with my brother and sisters,"
said Petey.

"All right, let's find a game for four players.
Then we can have three groups of four."

$$4 \times 3 = 12$$

"There are three balls here. Anyone for a game of four square?"

The kids formed squares and bounced the balls.

Corkscrew stole a ball, lay on his back, and juggled it. Pirate danced on top. They were a good team.

"Bad Corkscrew!"

"Bad Pirate!"

"You know, you'd think those animals were messing up our games on purpose."

That kid's not so dumb, thought Corkscrew.

"Let's all play one big game together."

"There are twelve of us, and we've already got a net up. We could make two teams of six."

$$6 \times 2 = 12$$

"How about volleyball? That takes six on a side."

The kids gathered, half on each side of the net.

What about us? In desperation Corkscrew ran across the yard and flung himself into the net. Pirate helped him get untangled.

"What's the matter with your pig?"

"He keeps getting in the way."

"So does your bird."

"Here's a Frisbee. Let's play Ultimate Frisbee. There's no way the animals can mess that up."

"But it takes seven for a team. So we'd need fourteen for two teams, and we only have twelve."

"We have thirteen if Corkscrew counts."

"And he ought to count; it's his birthday, after all."

"And fourteen if Pirate counts."

"Corkscrew's on our team," said Sally. "He can catch."

"But make sure Pirate can catch, too."

Hurrah! Corkscrew danced deliriously.
Pirate squawked with glee.

7 x 2 = 14

"I think that's what they wanted
all along."

"Happy birthday, Corkscrew."

"And everyone's invited to
my house next week for
Pirate's birthday party."

"Is it really Pirate's birthday next week?"
"Who knows. But I want another party."
"Pass the Frisbee."
"Catch, Corkscrew!"

"Good Pirate."

"Good Corkscrew."

Dear Readers, Big and Small,

To further explore the math concepts in this story, here are some additional questions and new activities to try. Have fun!

✳

Without Corkscrew and Pirate, the children at this party could group themselves evenly and all play these games at the same time, with no child left out or waiting in line: badminton, jump rope, four square, and volleyball. Could they all still have played those games if they had also included Corkscrew? Why?

✳

What would happen if each of the four children in the family had three guests, instead of two? How many children would be at the party? Could they group themselves evenly, with no child left out or waiting in line, to play badminton? Jump rope? Four square? Volleyball? Ultimate Frisbee? What could they play if they included Corkscrew and Pirate?

✳

Badminton can be played with any even number of players, since you play it in pairs—each player on one team being paired against a player on the opposite team. If you just answered above that badminton was possible, how many games could you set up at the same time where each team has the same number of players?

✳

It would have been difficult to include Corkscrew in this story without Pirate, because without Pirate the total number of possible players is 13. Why is 13 such a problematic number for this story?

✳

Is there any number of guests that each child in this family could have invited so that they could have played all five of the games in the story, with all children plus Corkscrew playing and no one waiting in line? What if they included both Corkscrew and Pirate? Why?

✳

Here's a fun activity: Gather a group of children and act out the story.